To anyone who ever felt like they didn't fit in, this book is for you.

Every child deserves to shine.

To Peter and my girls, thank you for your love and remarkable patience.

EMMA
AN ELEPHANT WITH EPILEPSY

Written by Jo North

Illustrated by Robert Hooper

Emma was very nervous. Today was the day she was starting at her new school, and she was worried what people would think of her.

Meeting new people was really hard for Emma; she had a condition called epilepsy which meant her brain behaved differently sometimes, and caused her arms and legs to do strange things she couldn't control.

Emma walked into the classroom and was greeted by Alice, Ollie and Dylan. "We've heard all about you!" said Alice, smiling at Emma.

"We've never had someone with epilepsy in our class before and we've all been taught what to do if your body starts doing weird stuff".

Emma went bright red, and wished the ground would swallow her up. She was so embarrassed. She hated the fact her epilepsy made her different to everyone else, and wished she could just feel normal.

Her new classmates were really kind to her and made her feel really welcome for the rest of the week, but Emma still felt very shy. She knew she was different and found it hard to relax.

The following week Emma woke up and didn't feel very well, so she didn't eat much breakfast. She got into school but still felt a bit funny, so sat quietly.

Halfway through maths, Ollie noticed Emma was just staring into space, which he remembered could be an early sign of an epileptic fit, so he told the teacher who sent the class out early for lunch.

Alice stayed behind with Ollie; they had both listened really well when they were told about Emma's epilepsy and they wanted to help their friend. Alice moved the chairs out of the way so Emma wouldn't hurt herself, and Ollie found a cushion to put under Emma's head.

The teacher then asked Alice and Ollie to go out to the playground so they wouldn't get upset. Emma began having a fit and the teacher put her in a safe position.

Emma fell asleep after her fit (they make her very tired) so Ollie and Alice came back in and sat next to her. When Emma woke up, she was very confused and Alice told her what had happened.

"Oh I'm sorry, how embarrassing", Emma mumbled, wishing she could just go home.

Alice gave her a cuddle. "Don't be silly, you don't need to be sorry at all. Ollie and I are your friends, and we will always help you." Emma looked up and Alice and Ollie grinned at her. They were very proud that they had been able to help Emma.

Emma smiled back at them - maybe having epilepsy wasn't so bad after all. She had lovely friends who had helped her, and she was no longer embarrassed around them. She also realised she hadn't had any food since breakfast, and she was starving! Emma got up slowly and grinned at Alice and Ollie. "What's for lunch then?"

The End

SHINE

More titles in the Shine series:

★ Dylan, a dog with dyslexia
★ Alice, an aardvark with autism
★ Ollie, an otter with OCD

9 781800 494831